NEEKA
AND
THE
SQUIRREL
HIGHWAY

Charlie Wes Harris

Illustrations by Daniel Majan

Archway Publishing books may be ordered through booksellers or by contacting:

Archway Publishing
1663 Liberty Drive
Bloomington, IN 47403
www.archwaypublishing.com
1 (888) 242-5904

Because of the dynamic nature of the Internet, any web addresses or links contained in this book may have changed since publication and may no longer be valid. The views expressed in this work are solely those of the author and do not necessarily reflect the views of the publisher, and the publisher hereby disclaims any responsibility for them.

Any people depicted in stock imagery provided by Thinkstock are models, and such images are being used for illustrative purposes only.
Certain stock imagery © Thinkstock.

Scripture taken from the New King James Version®. Copyright © 1982 by Thomas Nelson. Used by permission. All rights reserved.

ISBN: 978-1-4808-4560-2 (sc)
ISBN: 978-1-4808-4561-9 (hc)
ISBN: 978-1-4808-4559-6 (e)

Printed by Color House Graphics in the United States of America.

Archway Publishing rev. date: 7/28/2017

This book is dedicated to the memory of my parents, Leila (Magby) and John Wesley Harris, and to my five wonderful grandchildren

Daniel	Jaden
Rachel	Esther
Joseph Wesley	

I love each of you very much and all of you inspire and fill my heart and soul with happiness and joy. As God-loving children, may you grow into strong men and women of faith, grace and wisdom, with praise and honor to God our Savior.

•◆•

"I have no greater joy than to hear that
my children walk in truth."
<3 John 4>

Setting

With recent tragedies in France, Belgium, and the United States in 2015 and 2016, there is much concern about terror in the world. The story in this book is about terror in a child's world. It provides a fictionalized account of a true incident that occurred in the home of a family living in Baltimore, Maryland. The characters, including the squirrel, were living organisms.

Although this incident took place some years ago, the physical setting of its occurrence in west Baltimore remains in tact. The street mentioned in the story still exist by the same name. Grace and St. Peters School is now Wilkes School (since 2010) at Grace and St. Peters Episcopal Church. The relationship of the school and the church remains close. The teachers and administrators at the time of this story have passed on but their positions and titles are more or less the same today.

We cannot account for the whereabouts of the squirrel but the two little girls in this story have grown up, married, with families and children of their own. Obviously, there is evolutionary change in all communities and Baltimore is no exception.

Neeka loved to watch the pretty gray-brown squirrels in her yard when she was little. She liked the way they twitched their big fluffy tails in the wind as they ran up and down the tree-trunk. The squirrels didn't come to the yard often. But every once in a while Daddy would call her outside and say "Look who came to visit you, Baby!" Together, Neeka and Daddy would watch the two biggest squirrels play noisy games and chase each other in circles on the grass. Neeka's favorite had white fur on his belly and a red tail that turned to dark brown at the tip. The two squirrels were so fast they could scamper up the tree in just seconds. They could even jump from branch to branch, like fearless acrobats in a circus. Neeka thought they must be the bravest and strongest squirrels in all of her city of Baltimore!

When Neeka turned four, her family moved to a wide, shady street called Fernhill

Avenue. Neeka loved the quiet street, which was lined with tall old trees. The treetops met over the pavement and formed a green canopy that made a perfect mid-air squirrel playground. Once they were settled into their new house, Neeka got used to seeing squirrels everywhere. She forgot how exciting it used to be when the squirrels visited their old yard, and how Daddy would take her outside to watch them play. Neeka was a big girl now, five whole years old. She loved going to first grade at Grace and St. Peter's School. There were lots of interesting things to do there, and Neeka forgot all about the amazing acrobatic squirrels.

Early in the morning, Neeka and her Daddy would walk out to their blue Volvo sedan as a squirrel chattered at them from the low branch of a tree. Daddy drove Neeka to school every morning. As usual, Neeka was wearing her school uniform—a blue jumper with a white

Peter Pan collared blouse. She was wearing blue and white saddle oxfords and over-the-knee indigo stockings. It was chilly outside, so Neeka put on her red knit snuggle cap and gloves. Neeka's navy plaid coat had shiny gold buttons up the front. When he saw her in her cap and gloves, Daddy laughed and called her his Flag Girl. Neeka liked that, and she loved her winter colors of red, white and blue.

"Okay, Flag Girl, get in the car and buckle up," said Daddy.

The squirrel watched curiously as the Flag Girl got into the car. He chattered and chirped, and even leapt three feet to a branch that hung over the car. But the girl seemed busy and excited, and did not notice the squirrel, or even look up at all.

Daddy drove Neeka downtown to Grace and St. Peter's School. Along the way, Neeka

GRACE
and
ST. PETER'S
School

7

read all of the road signs out loud. Neeka had started attending Grace and St. Peter's when she was just in nursery school. Two years later, she knew the drive down Druid Hill Avenue so well she could read all the street-signs at a glance. Sometimes new signs appeared, and Neeka could read those too. Neeka loved her drives to school with Daddy. She liked the bright feeling of the morning, and the way Daddy always patted on her head when she read a sign, giving her a big smile of approval and saying, "that's right!" But Neeka's favorite thing of all was when she and Daddy would sing their favorite song together.

♪ *"Oh no, don't let the rain come down.* ♪
My roof's got a hole in it, and I might drown!"

When the song was over, Daddy patted her on the head again, smiling as he exclaimed,

"That was good, Baby!" Soon they were on spacious Park Avenue and at the drop-off lane in front of the school. Neeka picked up her book bag, holding the pretty pictures that she had cut out for today's "Show and Tell" carefully in one hand. Daddy got out and opened her door, but she waited. He leaned into the car and grinned. "Let's bail out!" he said. They both laughed. Daddy knew it was Neeka's favorite phrase, and she always waited for him to say it. Off Neeka went into her school. She cheerfully greeted all of her friends.

"Hi Dante! Hi Bryan! Look, I have on blue and white shoes, just like yours."

"Hi Francine! Hi Mark! Hi Kellye. Let's go outside and play on the jungle gym!

Soon Neeka was lining up with the other children to go back inside for classes and other school work. At her desk, she kept her mind on her work.

The teacher kept her very busy which made the day go by fast. Soon the school day was nearly over. The last period before going home was spent on the playground, a joyous time for Neeka but when she looked up and saw her teacher, Mrs. DeCampos, coming outside she knew it was time to go.

Neeka marched inside, took her seat in the lobby and waited to be picked up. As Neeka sat quietly waiting with a few other children, she thought of many things. First, about her best friend, Kellye, who was still playing outside, maybe skipping rope alone since Neeka was not there to play with her. It was too bad she couldn't wait on the playground, so she could play on the swings and watch her friends on the jungle gym. Neeka thought about her little baby sister, Gel (short for Angela) who she would see in a little while. Gel was a plump baby,

An Apple a day keeps the doctor away!

A message from the school management.

13

healthy and happy and round as a butterball. Neeka loved to see the pretty bright smile Gel always gave her when she got home from school.

At last Neeka heard her own name called, "Neeka Harris." She bowed, curtseyed while shaking hands with the dismissing teacher, Mrs. Myles-Hunkin, then walked quickly out of the door. Her Mommy was waiting for her in the car.

"Where is Daddy?" Neeka asked, as she climbed into the back seat and pulled the car door closed.

"Your Daddy had to go to a meeting," said Mommy. "So I came to pick you up instead.

"Fine!" Neeka replied as she rested her head against the back of the car seat, holding the toy that she was finally bringing home after leaving it at school several days for "Show and Tell."

15

Neeka had little to say on her way home. She never talked much on the way home from school. Today, she felt a little tired, and after all, she had done plenty of talking during the day. There was no playground at home, no jungle gym, and no friend nearby for Neeka to play with. It always seemed to Neeka that she was leaving all the fun behind when she left her school. So she was content to just sit quietly and rest her mind and body as she rode home.

Soon, Neeka was home. She took off her coat and cap and hung them in the closet just inside the front door. Suddenly, Neeka had a bright idea.

"I'll surprise my Daddy," she said to herself. "I'll arrange his shoes in his closet, clear off his table and hang the drawing I did at school today on his wall. I'll make Mommy's and Daddy's room look

neat and pretty, and he will be so pleased when he gets home."

Neeka hurried upstairs. Her Daddy would soon be home and there wasn't much time. She hadn't even reached the top of the stairs when she heard a key turn in the front door. Oh no! Daddy was home early from his meeting!

But Neeka knew her Daddy would stop downstairs to talk with her Mommy and play with Gel, the baby. She still had time to make the room look neat before he came upstairs.

When she got upstairs, Neeka opened the bedroom door and crept inside. She looked around, wondering where to start. Right away, she noticed there was something on the bed that didn't belong there. It looked like an old pair of brown wool socks.

"I'll just put those socks in the hamper," Neeka thought. She reached toward them, then

leapt back with a shriek when one of the socks twitched! Her heart pounding, Neeka crept closer, her eyes wide. That was *not* a pair of socks!

"It's a squirrel," Neeka whispered in disbelief. "But how can a squirrel be asleep on Mommy's and Daddy's bed?" The squirrel twitched again, eyes closed. He had fallen into a deep sleep on the comfortable bedding and was dreaming of a house made entirely of shelled nuts. The nuts smelled wonderful! In his sleep, the squirrel's nose began twitching.

"What is he doing?" Neeka wondered, as the squirrel's nose twitched and wriggled. She took a step closer, and a floorboard creaked. Suddenly, the squirrel's eyes opened. Neeka froze. The squirrel froze. Then the squirrel sprang from the bed and raced from corner to corner, looking for a way out. Then he leapt onto the window-sill. Outside was so close! The

squirrel frantically scratched and jumped, but he couldn't find a way through the cold shiny glass.

Neeka shrieked, and ran out of the room.

"Daddy! Oh Daddy, come quick!"

But what if the squirrel came after her?

Neeka ran down the hallway past the other rooms. She did not stop running until she reached the door to her bedroom all the way at the end of the hall. She ran inside and climbed up onto her chest of drawers. Surely the squirrel wouldn't get her up here! Her feet tucked under her, she began to yell again.

"Daddy! Daddy! Dadd-ee!" By this time, her Daddy was leaping up the stairs, three and

four steps at a time. He knew his daughter was in trouble and he was trying to get to her as fast as he could. Where was Neeka? He was not sure where her cries were coming from. Again, Neeka cried out, "Dadd-ee!"

Then he knew that Neeka was in her room. He burst through her door.

"What's the matter, Baby? What's the matter?" Neeka just pointed toward her parents' room.

"There is a squirrel in your room!" she cried. "How did it get there?"

Daddy thought for a moment.

"Well now, you remember that little chipmunk that climbed down the chimney last week? The one we caught in the little Have-a-Hart trap so we could let him outside?"

Neeka nodded, still clinging to the chest of drawers.

"Well, maybe that squirrel did the same thing."

"Baby, this squirrel made the journey down the chimney into our house." Daddy said, "In fact, maybe many squirrels have turned the chimney of our house into a highway." When the gray-brown squirrel came to the very end of the highway, there was light and he wanted to see what was there. So he decided to roam a bit. How interesting, he thought. He had found excitement! He loved walking around on the soft carpet of the living room. It was much like the grass outside but with a different smell. He walked carefully from one carpeted room to the next. Then he decided to go downstairs.

While downstairs, he spent a lot of time in the kitchen. Oh! What a pretty

room, he thought, gazing at its walls, painted yellow and white. his favorite colors. He looked in the icebox, the stove, and in the cupboard. He reached into the cabinet for a glass and poured himself a glass of cold orange juice. He drank it rapidly because he was thirsty.

After looking over the house downstairs, he made his way upstairs. In walking over the house, he looked closely at the furniture, stopping at every mirror, checking himself out to see if his face was looking handsome, and to smooth out any ruffles in his shiny fur. He paused for a long while looking at the paintings on the walls and at Neeka's drawings.

Neeka lived in a big house. The squirrel had walked all over it. He was tired when he reached her Daddy's room. So he decided to pause for a short rest. He climbed onto the bed to rest in comfort. He just wanted to relax but he did not plan to go to sleep. But within

a few minutes he was fast asleep.

"But why, Daddy, is this squirrel here?"

"Oh, he was probably just curious," Daddy said, his deep voice and wide smile relaxing Neeka. "What if you saw a tunnel or a highway that led up into the treetops – wouldn't you want to go have a peek? See what's up there?"

Neeka laughed, and nodded.

"Well, I'm sure the squirrel just wanted to do the same thing. Do you remember when we used to watch the big brown squirrels play at our old house?"

Neeka looked surprised. She had forgotten about those squirrels until just now.

"They were fun," Neeka said. "They chased each other, and they could run down a tree head first."

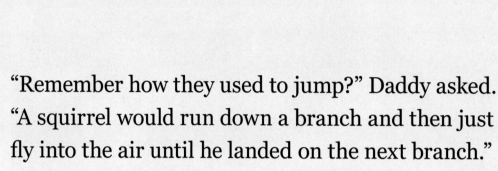

"Remember how they used to jump?" Daddy asked. "A squirrel would run down a branch and then just fly into the air until he landed on the next branch."

"I do remember," Neeka said, laughing. "It was like the tree was their playground, with monkey bars and a jungle gym and everything! Maybe he came through the squirrel highway to see if there was a playground inside our house!"

"Maybe he did," Daddy said. "Maybe he just wanted a friend. But you know what, Baby? That squirrel is probably scared now. We should try to help him get outside, so he can go back home."

Neeka hated to think the squirrel might be frightened. She hopped off the chest of drawers.

"I'll take you to him," she said. She felt a little brave, but took her father's hand so that she would feel even braver.

But when they reached the room, the squirrel was nowhere to be seen.

"He was right there, trying to get out the window," Neeka said.

"Well, he can't have gotten far," Daddy replied.

Under the bed, the trembling squirrel froze at the sight of Daddy's large feet. The girl was small and spoke softly, but this human must be very tall and very strong. With a powerful leap, the squirrel shot out from under the bed and sprang past Neeka's father and straight through the open bedroom doorway.

"There he goes!" Daddy exclaimed. "Your Mommy should open the front door."

"Mommy," Neeka shouted, running up the hallway toward the stairs. "Mommy, open the front door – there's a squirrel loose!"

Gel, the toddler, heard all of the commotion upstairs. She was on her way up, half crawling and pulling up by the rail on the side of the steps. She wanted to see what was going on with her sister. Gel was halfway up the stairs when the squirrel zoomed past her on his way down. She stood up quickly when she saw this furry blur speeding away. She was much too young to fear the squirrel like Neeka. She laughed and laughed and laughed as the squirrel rounded the stairs.

When the squirrel reached the bottom of the stairs, he immediately smelled fresh air.

Neeka's Mommy, Edna, had heard her daughter calling her to open the door, and had set the

front door wide open. Without looking back, the squirrel bounded through the door and sprinted across the lawn. He did not slow down until he reached his tree, which he scampered up.

Inside the house, everyone was talking at once. Mommy was telling Neeka and Daddy that she'd hidden behind a doorway to watch, and that she'd seen the squirrel run straight for his tree. Daddy said he would call a carpenter to put a screen over the chimney-top so other animals couldn't explore the highway. Gel laughed and in toddler talk said, "Rarebit! Ruin!"

"He's back in his tree now, Gel," said Daddy. "I think we gave him a bit of a scare."

"Poor thing probably had no idea what was happening," said Mommy. "He just came inside for a little visit."

Neeka looked up at the squirrel's tree. It made her feel sad to think she might have frightened the squirrel by screaming. When she first saw him asleep on the bed, with his white tummy and his fat tail with the black tip, he was sort of cute.

"Now he thinks we don't like him," Neeka thought.

She asked Mommy if she could have a cookie.

"Just one," Mommy said. "We'll be eating dinner soon."

Neeka wrapped the cookie in a napkin and walked outside. She crossed the lawn, and sat down at the base of the big old tree.

"I didn't mean to scare you," Neeka said softly. "When I was little, my Daddy and I used to watch squirrels playing near our house. I thought they were so wonderful – like little circus acrobats."

Neeka heard a chattering sound, and looked up. High above her, the squirrel was sitting on a branch, watching her with bright eyes.

"I love that your tree is your home and your playground," Neeka said. "Mine isn't like that, but I guess you know that since you've been inside it now."

The squirrel walked out along a thin branch, his eyes on Neeka. Just as it seemed the end of the limb was too flimsy to hold the squirrel, it dipped down under his weight and the squirrel neatly stepped onto the lower branch.

Neeka laughed.

"Oh, that's amazing!" she said. "It's like an escalator in a tree!"

The squirrel chirped, and swished his tail from side to side.

"Your tail is beautiful," Neeka said.

The sunlight was growing orange and pink, and the tree cast a long shadow. Neeka knew it was getting late.

"I have to go inside now," she said. "Maybe I can come back and see you again tomorrow."

The squirrel just watched her.

"I'm leaving a cookie for you," Neeka said. "It's a snickerdoodle – my favorite. I don't know if its good squirrel food though. Anyway, I'm sorry I scared you. See you later!"

Neeka got up and walked toward her house. When she reached the front door, she looked back.

The squirrel was sitting on the grass where Neeka had been, facing the house. He was sitting up on his hind legs, and he held the snickerdoodle between his two front paws. His eyes twinkled as he raised the cookie to his mouth and began to nibble on it.

Neeka smiled. The squirrel liked snickerdoodles too.

She opened the door and smelled the wonderful scents of dinner. Neeka felt very happy. She loved the Fernhill house, and was very glad they had moved there.

And it was beginning to look like she had a friend in the neighborhood after all.

When the family sat down for dinner, their talk was all about their exciting day – about their gray-brown visitor and his travels on the highway. For Neeka, her fear was gone but her memory of this day will be with her for the rest of her life..

The End

Real Life Characters
Neeka and Angela (Gel)